12/93

Dear Johnson Family,

Seek and ye
shall find ...
and have fun!

Remembering you
in prayer with
love in Christ,

Aunt
Renee

SAMMY'S INCREDIBLE TRAVELS

With
Jesus and His Friends

Titles
in

A Seeking Sammy Book

series:

Sammy's Fantastic Journeys
with the
Early Heroes of the Bible

Sammy's Incredible Travels
with
Jesus and His Friends

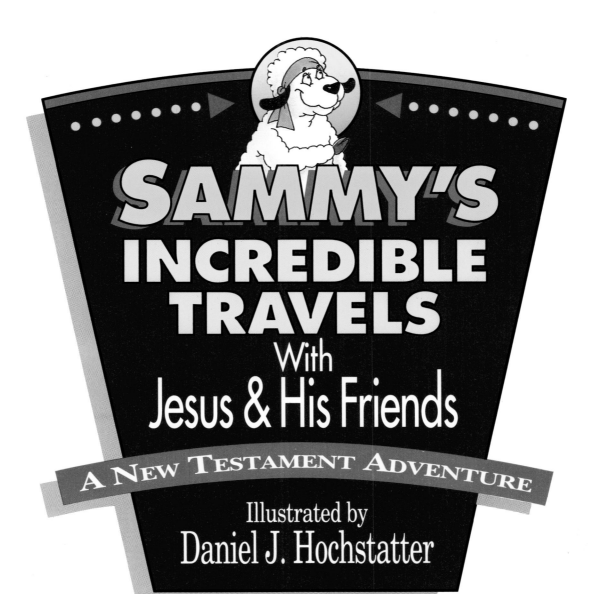

SAMMY'S INCREDIBLE TRAVELS

With Jesus & His Friends

A NEW TESTAMENT ADVENTURE

Illustrated by
Daniel J. Hochstatter

THOMAS NELSON PUBLISHERS
Nashville

Published in Nashville, Tennessee, by Oliver-Nelson Books, a division of Thomas Nelson, Inc., Publishers, and distributed in Canada by Lawson Falle, Ltd., Cambridge, Ontario.

The Bible version used in this publication is THE NEW KING JAMES VERSION. Copyright © 1979, 1980, 1982, Thomas Nelson, Inc., Publishers.

Printed in the United States of America

ISBN 0–8407–9162–3

1 2 3 4 5 6 —97 96 95 94 93 92

SAMMY'S
INCREDIBLE TRAVELS
With Jesus and His Friends

> ## *It all started because . . .*

I am a shepherd boy. I spend many days and nights in the hills taking care of my sheep. Usually I am out there all alone. Sometimes I miss having someone to talk with.

One of the lambs, Sammy, stays close by me. We have become good friends. When I get really bored I like to sit and tell Sammy a story. Now I know a sheep cannot understand what I am saying, but sometimes I wonder . . .

I like Bible stories most of all. As I tell what happened in each story, I see Sammy looking off into space. He seems to be imagining how it might have been. I wonder if Sammy and I are in the pic-tures along with all the characters—heroes like Paul, Silas, and even Jesus Himself. I wonder what else Sammy sees in those pictures.

See if you can find Sammy and me in the pictures that follow. Join us in our adventures. And while you're at it, see how many crazy things you can find. There are some at the bottom of each page. If you get really good, try to find the ones listed on the page at the end of the book.

Find Sammy, the Shepherd, and as many of these things as you can.

 White Dove

 Party Sheep

 Sheep Angel

 Party Angel

THE SHEPHERDS SEE ANGELS

—Luke 2:8-16

Some shepherds were watching over their sheep in a field outside Bethlehem. It was a quiet, peaceful night, and they were relaxing after a busy day.

Suddenly the peace was shattered by an angel who appeared in the sky. "Do not be afraid," the angel said. "For there is born to you this day in the city of David a Savior, who is Christ the Lord. . . . You will find a Babe wrapped in swaddling cloths, lying in a manger." Then a whole choir of angels appeared and sang, "Glory to God in the highest, and on earth peace, goodwill toward men!"

After the angels left, the shepherds hurried into Bethlehem to see this wonderful new baby!

Bald Angel

Pizza Angel

Find Sammy, the Shepherd, and as many of these things as you can.

 Rope Walker

 Backward Rider

 Balloon Man

 Taxi

THE MISSING BOY

—Luke 2:41-51

Mary and Joseph went to Jerusalem every year to celebrate the Feast of the Passover. When Jesus was twelve years old, He went along.

When the feast was over, everyone began the trip home. Mary and Joseph were walking along with many other people. Jesus wasn't with His parents, but they thought He was probably walking with His cousins or friends. After a whole day of walking they still hadn't seen Jesus, and so they asked a few people about Him. No one had seen Him.

Mary and Joseph went back to Jerusalem. They looked for three days and finally found Jesus in the temple. He was talking with the teachers and asking them questions. Everyone was surprised at how much He understood. Then Jesus went home with His parents because He always obeyed them.

Catch This

Pet Piggy

Find Sammy, the Shepherd, and as many of these things as you can.

 Dancing Sheep

 Fish Flipping

 Jumbo Hot Dog

 Boy with Sunglasses

THE FIRST MIRACLE

—*John 2:1-11*

Jesus and His disciples were invited to a wedding in Cana, a small village in Galilee. Jesus' mother was there too. During the celebration the host ran out of wine to serve the guests. Jesus' mother knew that He could help, so she told the servants to do whatever Jesus asked.

Jesus told the servants to fill six big jars with water. Then He told them to pour some of the water out of the jars. When they did so, they discovered that Jesus had turned the water into wine. This was the first time Jesus did a miracle, and it showed who He was.

Man on Stilts

Tightrope Mouse

Find Sammy, the Shepherd, and as many of these things as you can.

 Drumstick

 Whistler

 Pizza Man

 Woman with Bird

A SICK MAN DROPS IN

—Mark 2:1-5

Jesus came to Capernaum to speak about God. So many people wanted to hear Him that the house where He was staying was packed with people.

Four men brought a friend of theirs who was paralyzed. They knew that Jesus could heal their friend if only they could get him close to Jesus. They tried to go in through the door of the house, but they couldn't get past the crowd. Then the four men thought of another plan. They took their sick friend up to the flat roof of the house and began to tear away the roof. They made a hole just big enough to lower their friend through.

As Jesus was speaking, the men lowered the paralyzed man down through the roof right in front of Him. Jesus saw how much faith the men had, and so He healed their friend and even forgave his sins.

Very Long Beard

Upset Woman

Find Sammy, the Shepherd, and as many of these things as you can.

 Sheep Catching Oranges

 Red Balloon

 Burger Man

 Squirrel on Swing

JESUS BY THE SEA OF GALILEE

—Matthew 4:18-20; Mark 3:7-11; Luke 5:4-6

Jesus often walked along the shore near the Sea of Galilee. Hundreds of people came out from the villages to hear Him teach. Many of them were sick or blind or crippled and wanted Jesus to heal them. He was always loving, kind, and patient with these people.

Jesus did all sorts of things by the sea. He helped the disciples catch fish there. He also called men to follow Him there. The people who loved Jesus had good memories of times spent with Him near the sea.

Water Fountain Man

Man in Cool Shades

Find Sammy, the Shepherd, and as many of these things as you can.

 Fish Sandwich

 Fish Heads

 Man in Tree

 Skipped Fish

JESUS FEEDS A HUNGRY CROWD

—Luke 9:11-17; John 6:1-14

Jesus had been teaching all day. Thousands of people had come to hear Him talk about God's kingdom. Now it was supper time, and the disciples thought Jesus should send the people away to eat.

But Jesus had a better idea. He had the disciples search through the crowd for anyone with food. They found one boy who had brought a lunch of five loaves of bread and two small fish. The little boy was happy to give his food to Jesus.

Jesus took the food and blessed it. Then the disciples passed it out to the crowd. More than five thousand people ate all they wanted that day, and there were even leftovers!

Bread and Butter

Balanced Diet

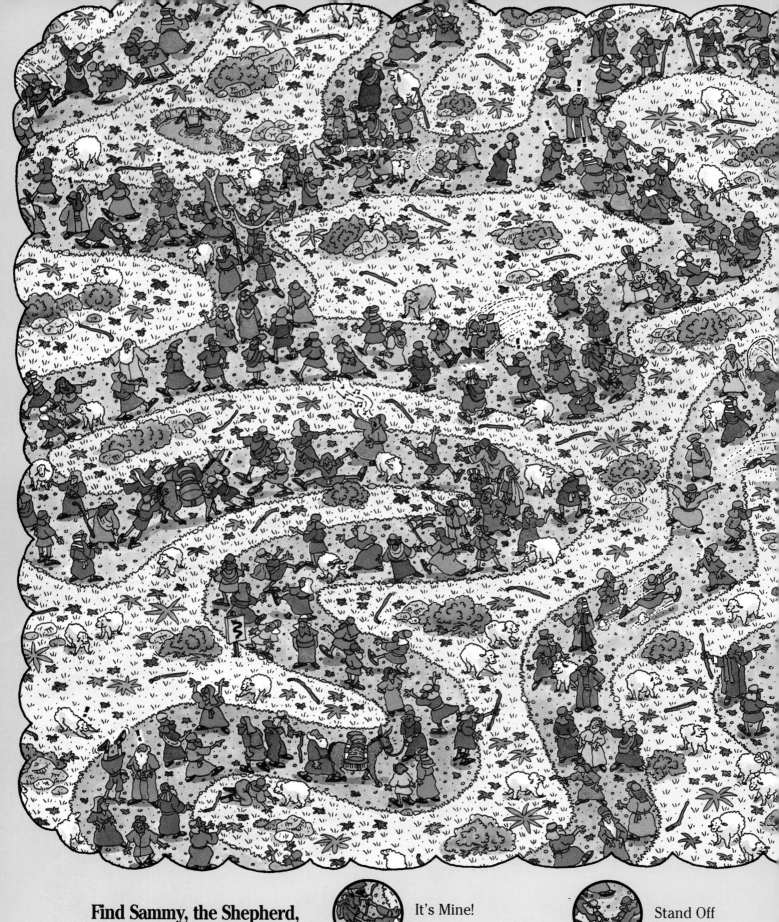

Find Sammy, the Shepherd, and as many of these things as you can.

 It's Mine!

 Stand Off

 Bread Thrower

 Short Cut

A MAN IN A TREE

—Luke 19:1-8

One time Jesus was passing through Jericho where a man named Zacchaeus lived. Zacchaeus was a tax collector, and sometimes he took more money than he should have from people. Zacchaeus wanted to see the teacher he had heard so much about. But he had a problem—he was a short man, and crowds of people lined the streets. He would never be able to see over them, and no one would let him through.

Suddenly Zacchaeus noticed a sycamore tree next to the road. That gave him an idea! He climbed the tree and had a bird's-eye view of Jesus coming down the road. When Jesus passed by, He called, "Zacchaeus, make haste and come down, for today I must stay at your house."

After Jesus and Zacchaeus talked for a while, Zacchaeus decided to give half his goods to the poor and to pay back four times what he owed to anyone from whom he had stolen.

Hot Dog Snack

Very Long Beard

Find Sammy, the Shepherd, and as many of these things as you can.

 Man on a Swing

 Sheep with a View

 Tree Climber

 Bird Man

JESUS RIDES INTO JERUSALEM

—*Mark 11:1-10*

Jesus and His disciples had been walking for many days, and now they were near Jerusalem. But Jesus stopped along the road and sent two disciples on an errand. He asked them to go into a nearby village. They would find a donkey colt tied there. They were to borrow the colt for Him to ride.

The disciples brought the colt to Jesus, and He rode it toward Jerusalem. Crowds of people lined the streets and waved palm branches as He rode by. Some even laid their coats down on the road in front of Jesus. The people followed Him to the city shouting, "Hosanna! Blessed is He who comes in the name of the LORD! . . . Hosanna in the highest!"

JERUSALEM CLEANERS

3 Peeking Sheep

Man on a Ladder

Find Sammy, the Shepherd, and as many of these things as you can.

 Smooching Sheep

 Singing Soldier

 Camera Bug

 2-Spear Soldier

JESUS is BETRAYED

—Mark 14:32-46

Jesus knew that His time on earth was nearly over. He took some of His disciples to the Garden of Gethsemane. He needed to pray, and He wanted His friends to be close by. All of the disciples were there except Judas.

While Jesus was speaking with His disciples, a crowd came into the garden carrying swords and clubs. Judas was leading them. He walked right up to Jesus and kissed Him on the cheek. This kiss was a signal for the others in the crowd, and they grabbed Jesus and arrested Him.

Pizza Man

Sheep in Shades

Find Sammy, the Shepherd, and as many of these things as you can.

 Side–Mounted Man

 Sheep with Ball and Chain

 3 Blind Mice

 Shirtless Soldier

PAUL AND SILAS IN JAIL

—Acts 16:16-34

Paul and Silas were in jail because they had cast a spirit out of a slave girl who told fortunes. The Romans were so angry with them that they beat them and put them in an inner cell. They didn't take any chances on Paul and Silas escaping.

Paul and Silas sang hymns and prayed that night as the other prisoners listened. Suddenly, around midnight, the floor and the walls began to shake. A strong earthquake shook the doors open, and the chains fell off all the prisoners. The jailer thought all his prisoners had escaped, and he started to kill himself. Paul stopped him by shouting, "Do yourself no harm, for we are all here."

The jailer was so impressed that he asked Paul and Silas how to be saved. They told him to believe in Jesus, and that very night the jailer and his whole family were baptized.

Small Door

Upside-Down Prisoner

Find Sammy, the Shepherd, and as many of these things as you can.

 Strong Man

 Stick–Em–Up

Woman with Bird

 Bar–B–Q

PAUL SPEAKS IN ATHENS

—Acts 17:16-32

Paul was in Athens teaching about Jesus, and he noticed that the people there worshiped strange gods instead of the one true God. He talked with some of the people about this, and they invited him to go to the Areopagus—a hill where they met—to speak with the council.

When Paul spoke there he said, "Men of Athens, I perceive that in all things you are very religious; for as I was passing through and considering the objects of your worship, I even found an altar with this inscription: TO THE UNKNOWN GOD. Therefore, the One whom you worship without knowing, Him I proclaim to you . . . Lord of heaven and earth."

The men of the council listened to Paul speak, and when he was finished, some of them asked to hear more about God.

Tightrope Walker

Bread Kicker

Find Sammy, the Shepherd, and as many of these things as you can.

 Triple Scoopers

 Hot Dogs

 Melon Man

 Pizza Man

THE RIOT AT EPHESUS

—*Acts 19:23-41*

Paul and his friends were traveling around telling people to worship only the one true God—not the idols that were so popular. This made some people in Ephesus very angry.

One man named Demetrius made his living by building silver shrines of the goddess Diana. Demetrius began stirring up the people against Paul. He said Paul was going to ruin their businesses and take away their income. Soon the whole city was in an uproar. Two of Paul's companions were seized to be put on trial.

Finally the city clerk calmed the screaming crowd. He told Demetrius and the others that if they had a problem with Paul they should go to the courts. They could not take the law into their own hands.

Skateboard Man

Sticky Situation

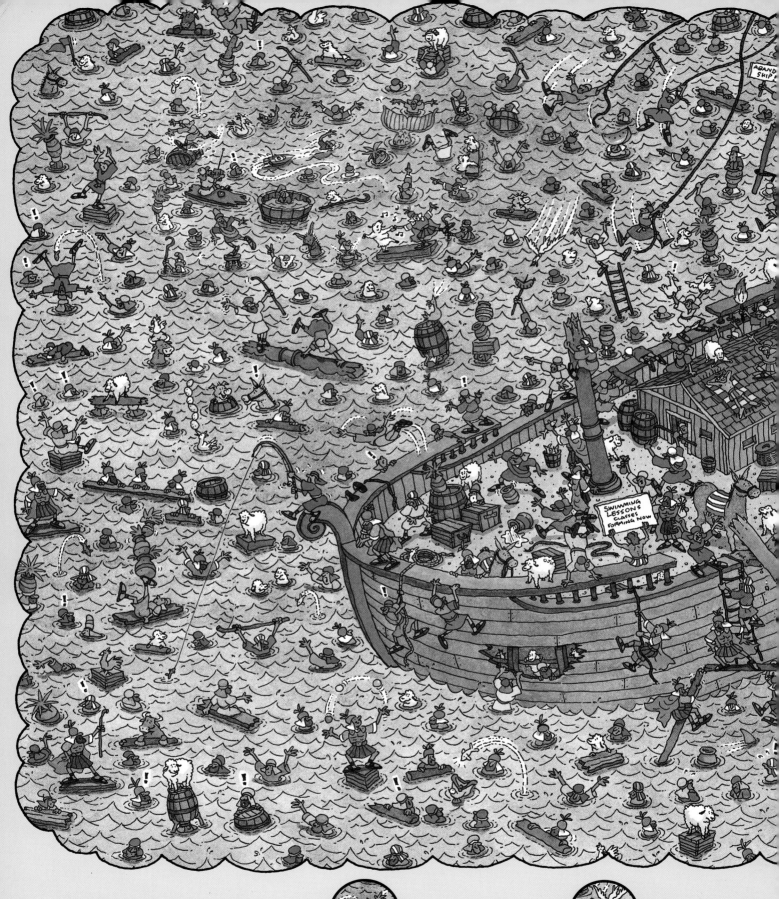

Find Sammy, the Shepherd, and as many of these things as you can.

 Swan Dive

 Free Lunch

 Peaceful Old Man

 Nice Catch

PAUL IS SHIPWRECKED

—*Acts 27:13-44*

Paul had been taken prisoner in Jerusalem, and he asked to be tried before Caesar in Rome. Now he and some other prisoners were on a ship that was sailing for Italy.

Before long, a terrible storm blew up. Some of the sailors were frightened and wanted to abandon ship. But Paul—with the soldiers' help—convinced everyone to stay and even to eat so they would be strong. The crew did as Paul said. Then they began to throw some things overboard to try to save the ship. But the ship ran aground that morning, and the strong waves began pounding it and breaking it into pieces.

Some of the soldiers wanted to kill the prisoners on board, but the centurion wouldn't let them. He wanted Paul to be safe. Instead everyone jumped overboard and swam or floated safely to shore.

Bad Balance

Seafood Snack

SEEKING SAMMY

See how many crazy things you can find

THE SHEPHERDS SEE ANGELS
1. Strong Angel
2. Mouse Angel
3. Wiener Roaster
4. Radio
5. Bone
6. Chicken Drumstick
7. Angel Reading Book
8. Mouse
9. Upside–Down Angel
10. Wingless Angel
11. Angel in Sunglasses

THE MISSING BOY
1. Bar of Soap
2. Birdhouse
3. Cross Country Skier
4. Sunbather
5. Lost Shorts
6. Money Sack
7. Man Slipping on Banana Peel
8. Sheep Walking Donkey
9. Spaghetti Man
10. Sledgehammer

THE FIRST MIRACLE
1. Giraffe
2. Very Tall Man
3. Man Doing Cartwheel
4. Girl Twirling Baton
5. Man on Sled
6. Man in Barrel
7. Radio
8. Man in Manhole
9. Big Bowling Ball
10. Sunbather
11. Woman Reading Book

A SICK MAN DROPS IN
1. Snorkeler
2. Loaf of Bread
3. Bird on Man's Shoulder
4. Kick-Me Sign
5. Juggler
6. Smoochers
7. Hot Tea
8. Attractive Woman
9. Woman Holding Fish
10. Party Man
11. Cowboy

JESUS BY THE SEA OF GALILEE
1. Barrel of Monkeys
2. Man Holding 2 Doves
3. Snake
4. Coconut Shaker
5. Woman Holding Fish

6. Man Giving Woman Flower
7. Ricochet Rock
8. Wind-Blown Hat
9. White Envelope
10. Man with Shovel
11. Book

JESUS FEEDS A HUNGRY CROWD
1. 5-Man Loaf
2. 2-Man Fish
3. Man Hiding in Basket
4. Sheep Throwing Bread
5. Fish Juggler
6. Snoozer
7. Shirtless Man
8. Man Balancing 3 Baskets of Bread
9. Sheep in Basket
10. Sheep on Man's Back
11. 2-Point Bread

A MAN IN A TREE
1. Singing Woman
2. Z Stick
3. 2 Men Pushing Donkey
4. Man Doing Splits
5. Hot Coffee
6. Sheep with Staff in Mouth
7. Snoozer
8. White Dove on Man's Head
9. Rope Skipper
10. Underwater Headstand
11. Woman with Flag

JESUS RIDES INTO JERUSALEM
1. Singing Man
2. Clothesline
3. Pizza Man
4. Weather Vane
5. Bone
6. Man Selling Palms
7. Street Sign
8. Man Bowing Down on Knees
9. Very Long Beard
10. Man Standing on Stool
11. Falling Coconut

JESUS IS BETRAYED
1. Twin Torch
2. Golfer
3. 3-Man Spear
4. Sheep in Tree
5. 2-Headed Spear
6. Small Torch
7. Sheep Fountain
8. Soldier Roasting Wiener

9. Bone
10. Teeter–Totter

PAUL AND SILAS IN JAIL
1. Very Long Beard
2. Tightrope Mouse
3. Prisoner Carrying Wood Box
4. Pizza Man
5. Wall–Shackled Sheep
6. Diver
7. Wall Clock
8. Snapped Whip
9. Bowling Ball
10. Sheep in Hole
11. Man Standing on Another Man's Shoulders

PAUL SPEAKS IN ATHENS
1. Barrel of Monkeys
2. Christmas Tree
3. Hot Cup of Coffee
4. Very Long Beard
5. Man on Unicycle
6. Pizza Man
7. Maps for Sale
8. Baseball Fan
9. Hot Dog on Stick
10. Man Throwing Frisbee
11. Tennis Racket

THE RIOT AT EPHESUS
1. Flower Man
2. Statue on Skateboard
3. Giant Sub Sandwich
4. Woman with Long Hair
5. Kite
6. Mismatched Boxers
7. Snoozer
8. Big–Winded Man
9. Red Balloon
10. Basketball
11. Pink Pig

PAUL IS SHIPWRECKED
1. Hen Balancing 6 Eggs
2. Big Fish Fin
3. Fisher
4. Radio-Controlled boat
5. Man Standing on Stool
6. Sunbather
7. Man on Swing
8. Snorkeler
9. 4 Men Holding Log
10. Watermelon
11. Man Holding 2 Hens